For Great Dividers everywhere
D. D.

To my family
and Dixie and Grover
T. M.

First published 2000 by Walker Books Ltd
87 Vauxhall Walk, London SE11 5HJ

2 4 6 8 10 9 7 5 3 1

Text © 2000 Dayle Ann Dodds
Illustrations © 2000 Tracy Mitchell

This book has been typeset in Handwriter.

Printed in Hong Kong

British Library Cataloguing in Publication Data
A catalogue record for this book is
available from the British Library.

ISBN 0-7445-5624-4

Y DOD
Countries
CF

The Great Divide

A mathematical marathon

∿

Written by
Dayle Ann Dodds

Illustrated by
Tracy Mitchell

WALKER BOOKS
AND SUBSIDIARIES
LONDON • BOSTON • SYDNEY

"BANG!" GOES THE GUN. THE RACE IS ON.

A CLOUD OF DUST. THEY'RE HERE – THEY'RE GONE...

Pushing and pedalling side by side,

eighty begin The Great Divide.

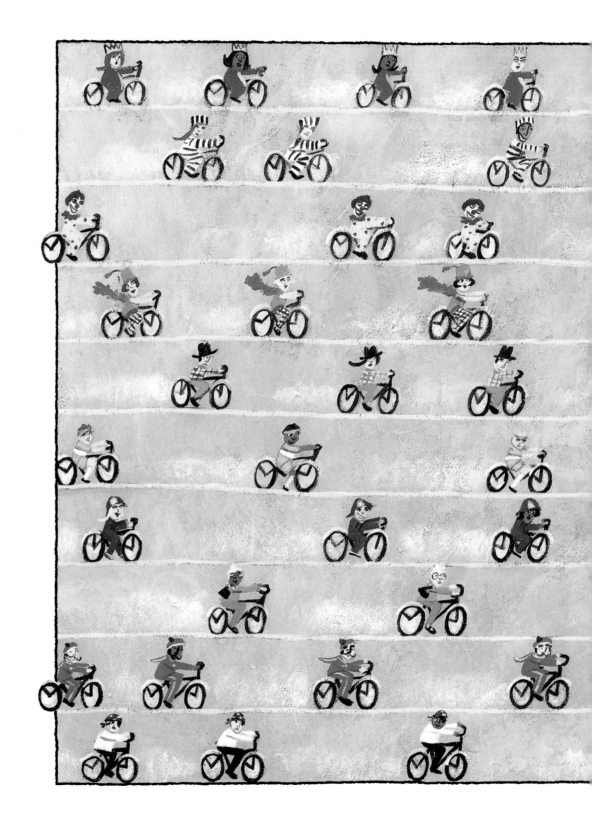

Just up ahead, just beyond sight,
one path leads left,
one path leads right.

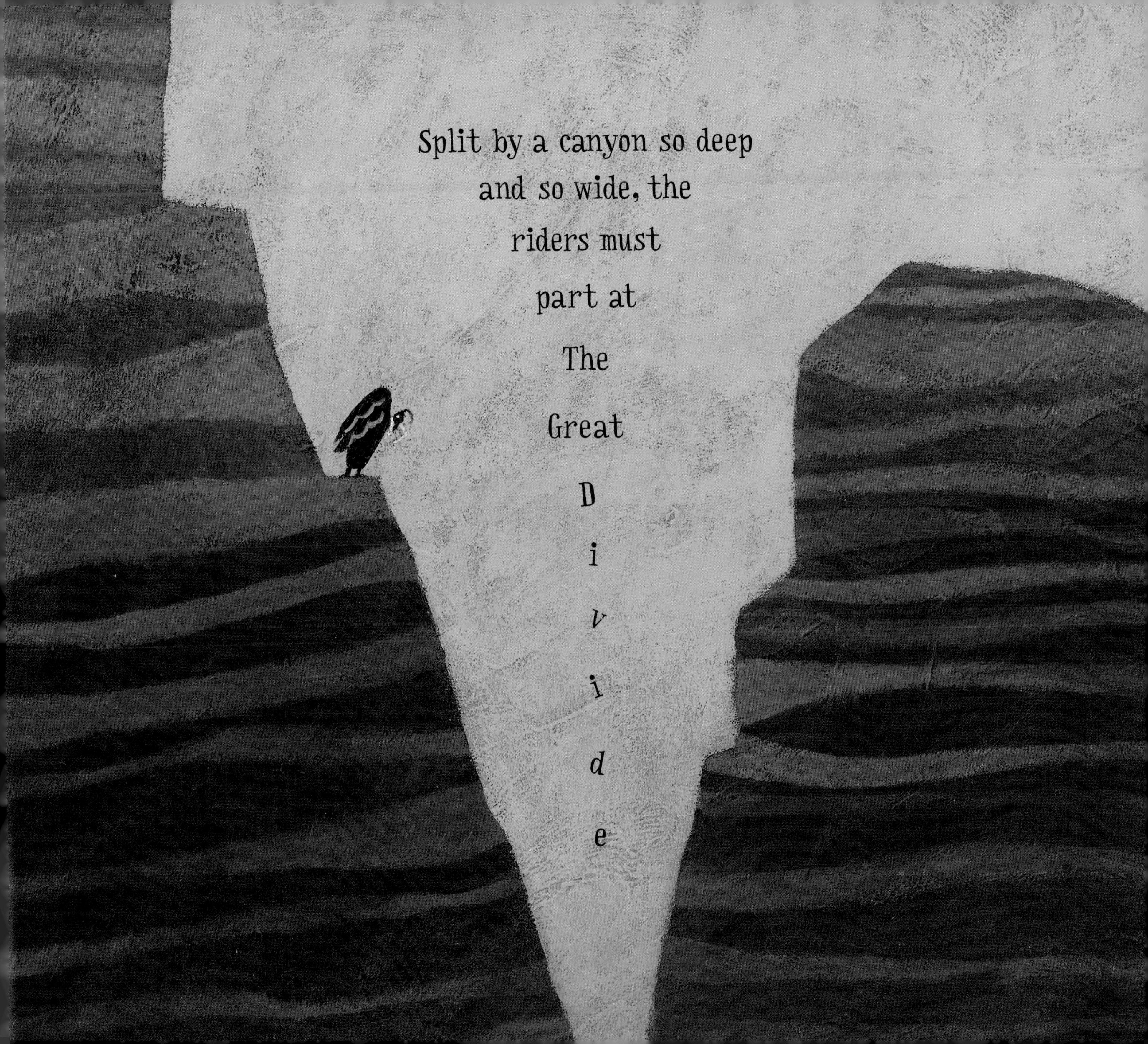

Split by a canyon so deep
and so wide, the

riders must

part at

The

Great

D

i

v

i

d

e

Half blunder left,
where their tyres go

pop!

Half hurtle right,
never to stop.

Help! Help!

On with the race.
Head for a boat!

Forty racers
now have to float!

What's up ahead?
A loud, roaring sound!
Whooshing whirlpools
spin all around.

Half are swept up
in a dizzying whirl.
Half battle on through
foam and swirl.

Out of the river,
on to dry land,

twenty racers
take to the sand.

One path turns east.
One path turns west.
Split by a mountain,
which choice is best?

Half stampede west
to a muddy disgrace.
Half gallop east
at a thunderous pace.

In hot-air balloons
floating up high,

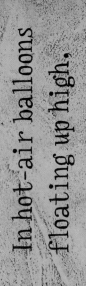

ten racers
now sail through
the sky!

Half blow north
right into a storm.
Half breeze south,
safe and warm.

5

Five press on,
pushing danger aside,
determined to win
The Great Divide.

Into the city,
down the main street,
they're racing on foot—
they're in a dead heat.

One runner stops
with a stone in her shoe.

Four are now left,
split two and two.

Pedalling bicycles –
one to each pair –
they zoom on ahead
as fast as they dare.

So fast, in fact, they
can't find the brake.
With a crash
and a splash
they fall in the lake!

FINISH

A hush fills the crowd.
They look far.
They look near.
Are there no racers left?
Have they no one to cheer?

LINE!

Are there zero left over?
Are there nought?
Are there none?
Not one? Not any?
Is the race done?

Wait!

Up in the sky –
what could it be?
Roaring!
Soaring!
Who do they see?

With a wave
    of her hand,
        with a dip
            and a glide,

1

ONE
CROSSES!
SHE WINS
THE GREAT
DIVIDE!

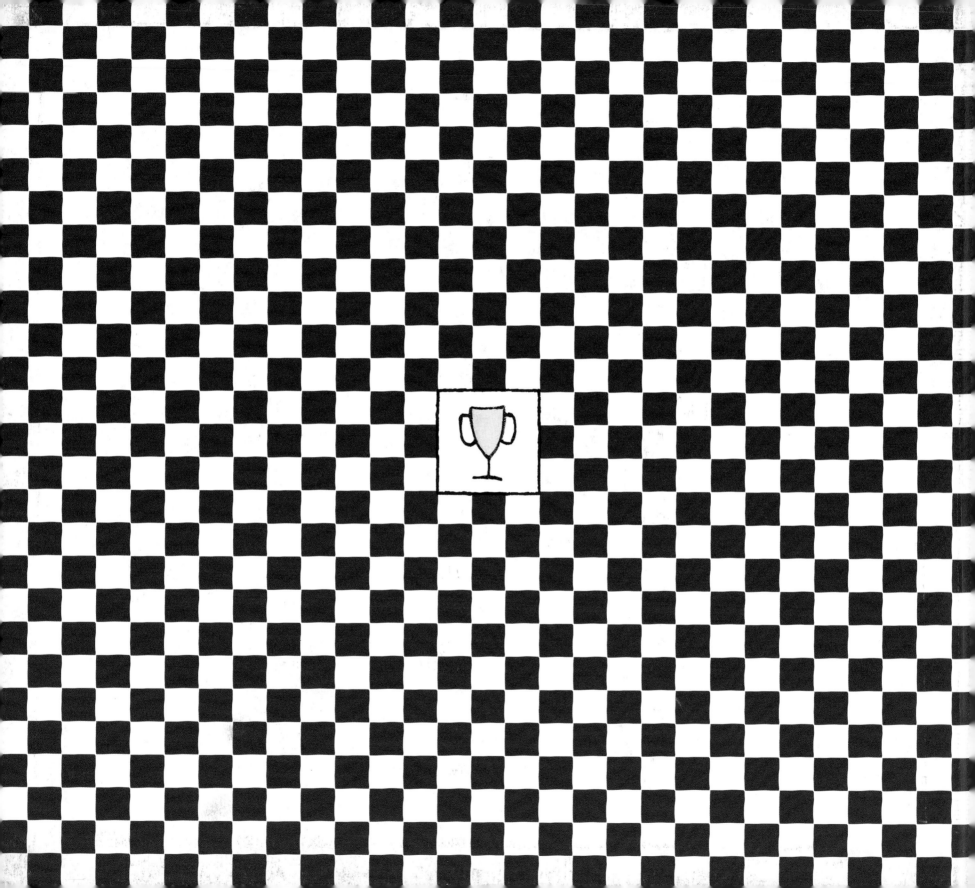